W9-BIV-010

"There's a pony in there!"

I'm in the truck, beside the pony. Her golden eyes roll wildly. She struggles to get up, but the rope holds her down.

People climb in with me. A knife cuts the rope and the pony lurches up. Scared wild, she's all set to gallop out of the truck. I catch her rough rope halter and hang on.

Jinny's got the other side of the halter. Together we ease the pony down onto the road. Jinny says, "She doesn't look hurt." And she doesn't. She looks terrified and battered, but not even her slender legs seem injured.

The driver plods up beside us. He looks at me. "You got shomeplace t' keep it?" His missing tooth makes talking hard.

Of course I haven't any place to put her, but I nod eagerly. Jinny nods, too.

He mouths, "Okay. Keep it."

"Keep it? You mean for always?"

He nods. "Dog meat," he explains. "Jush dog meat. Keep it."

Books by Anne Eliot Crompton

The Rainbow Pony
The Snow Pony

Available from MINSTREL Books

For orders other than by individual consumers, Minstrel
Books grants a discount on the purchase of **10 or more**
copies of single titles for special markets or premium use.
For further details, please write to the Vice-President of
Special Markets, Pocket Books, 1230 Avenue of the Ameri-
cas, New York, NY 10020.

For information on how individual consumers can place
orders, please write to Mail Order Department, Paramount
Publishing, 200 Old Tappan Road, Old Tappan, NJ
07675.

THE RAINBOW PONY

Anne Eliot Crompton

A MINSTREL® BOOK

PUBLISHED BY POCKET BOOKS

New York   London   Toronto   Sydney   Tokyo   Singapore

The sale of this book without its cover is unauthorized. If you purchased this book without a cover, you should be aware that it was reported to the publisher as "unsold and destroyed." Neither the author nor the publisher has received payment for the sale of this "stripped book."

This book is a work of fiction. Names, characters, places and incidents are products of the author's imagination or are used fictitiously. Any resemblance to actual events or locales or persons, living or dead, is entirely coincidental.

A MINSTREL PAPERBACK *Original*

 A Minstrel Book published by
POCKET BOOKS, a division of Simon & Schuster Inc.
1230 Avenue of the Americas, New York, NY 10020

Copyright © 1995 by Anne Eliot Crompton

All rights reserved, including the right to reproduce
this book or portions thereof in any form whatsoever.
For information address Pocket Books, 1230 Avenue
of the Americas, New York, NY 10020

ISBN: 0-671-51121-1

First Minstrel Books printing July 1995

10 9 8 7 6 5 4 3 2 1

A MINSTREL BOOK and colophon are registered trademarks
of Simon & Schuster Inc.

Front cover illustration by Deb Hoeffner

Printed in the U.S.A.

For Will Crompton,
my husband and best friend

June 28
9 A.M.

Hey, Alice!" says Jinny O'Neal on the phone.

"Hi, Jinny." I duck away from the receiver. Jinny's bright, cheery voice carries extra well.

"I'm going baby-sitting. Want to come?"

My heart sinks. "You mean at Taylors'?"

"Blast off. But it's good money. Taylors always pay right up."

That's fine for Jinny. They pay Jinny, not me. I say, "I'll call you back."

I hang up and call, "Grandma? Grandma!"

Grandma is deafer than she used to be. She doesn't hear me. I hear rattle and clink in the kitchen, so I go in there. She's shelving the dishes I just washed. Small, neat, and gray like a Siamese cat, she's standing on a chair to reach the higher shelves.

"Grandma," I say loudly, "Jinny called."

"What say?" Grandma looks around to read my lips. "That Jinny O'Neal up at the farm?"

"Right. She wants me to baby-sit with her."

"For pay?" Right away Grandma asks that!

"Well, actually . . ."

"You know that's not fair."

I mumble, "Yes. But there's nothing doing around here."

"What say, Alice?"

Loudly. "There's not much to do here."

"Not much to do! Promised land! You can vacuum, polish, sort, iron—take your pick!" Watching my face, Grandma giggles. "Go on, baby-sit for free if you want to. Wear your oldest jeans and a raincoat."

"Raincoat?"

"Radio says rain. My wrists say it, too." Grandma claims her arthritis forecasts weather better than the radio.

"Okay, I'll call Jinny back." Even baby-sitting for free at Taylors' sounds better than vacuuming, polishing, sorting. . . .

I call Jinny, say "Okay," then run upstairs for my oldest jeans. They make sense for going anywhere at all with Jinny. But I leave the raincoat on its hook in the closet. It's too bulky and hot for comfort.

My room is big enough for my bed, bureau, and homework desk. I throw the pink bedspread over the rumpled blankets so Grandma won't feel she has to make the bed and run back downstairs.

I wait for Jinny on the front porch. Maybe I should rethink that raincoat. Black and gray clouds boil around the sky.

Granton, Massachusetts, crouches under O'Neal's Hill. I can see the whole town from here. Our house is halfway up O'Neal Road. A steep dirt road leads past us and up to the O'Neal farm on the hilltop.

I know that right now, up at the farm, Jinny is whistling for her old black pony, Jet. Up he trots, hoping for a carrot. I hope she gives him one. Now she bridles him, scrambles aboard, and nudges his round side with one torn sneaker.

Jet nods, paws once at the dirt, and steps out.

He plods gently past laundry blowing on the line and chickens scratching in the yard, and turns down O'Neal Road toward me. I see it all happening as though I'm right there.

Bingo! I hear hoofbeats and Jinny's tuneless whistle. Jinny and Jet round the bend and pause at our gate, which is half-hidden behind Dad's tall, strong summer flowers. (They aren't in bloom yet, of course. Right now they look like a tangle of wild weeds.)

Jet is a big old pony, almost a horse. His black coat is gray-sprinkled, like my dad's black hair. His eyes are dark and kind.

Jinny is freckled and thin, with sharp angles. Her carrot red ponytail swings to her waist. My brown ponytail pokes between my shoulders. She reaches a hand to help me climb up Jet.

This is not easy, with no saddle to hold on to. I grab Jinny's hand and jump, catch Jet's well-padded spine, and wriggle up his side. Then I wrap my arms around Jinny's skinny waist. Jet moves out, and we swing slowly down the dirt road.

I love Jet's comfortable horse smell. I love his broad, safe back and the soft thud of his unshod hoofs on dirt. I would give the world and the moon for a pony like Jet.

My dad has a NO ANIMALS rule. Even Grandma, his own mother, can't keep the cat she wants so much. "Animals eat," Dad says. Well, sure they do. "That costs. Then they get worms and have to see the vet. I don't want to tell you what *that* costs! We're having NO ANIMALS at our house." Inside or outside.

Dad works in Granton down below us, at Granton Tire and Tube. He got a big raise last year, when I was ten. That's when we moved up here to O'Neal's Hill. Before that we lived in an apartment down in Granton on River Road. If Jet stood still so I could see, I could point to it from here. Down there in town the NO ANIMALS rule maybe made sense, but not up here. A pony can just graze free all over O'Neal's Hill all summer. Jet does.

Taylors' is the first house we come to under the hill. We slide down Jet. Jinny unbridles him and turns him loose in their fenced-in yard. As we walk to the porch the clouds burst.

Those boiling black and gray clouds just let go. Rain drums down like Niagara Falls. Jet shies. Then he droops, head low, and lets the rain run off him. We run indoors.

It's a rainy Taylor day. Taylors' is bad enough when the sun shines and the kids are outside! We crunch plastic toys underfoot, change diapers, build blocks, knock them down, watch cartoons, spread peanut butter, pour milk, mop up milk, for three kids under six.

It seems like three days later when the Taylors come home. Actually, it's three o'clock. Jinny pockets her money. The Taylors always pay on time. That's why we come here whenever they want. We wave a happy goodbye to the kids and walk out.

Jinny says, "Hey, it stopped!"

Rain drips from roofs, not from the sky.

Jinny says, "Hey, this mud is like ice!" She hangs on to the porch railing and slides down the steps.

A rattling pickup roars around the bend, too fast for this slippy mud. The brakes try to brake. The truck squeals, jerks, shudders, shies, turns nose to tail, and flops on its side. There's a cosmic crash and a shriek.

You see stuff like this on TV, not in real life. Glued to the porch rail, I stand and stare.

Jinny runs, slipping and sliding, toward the truck.

Taylors burst out the door past me and run to the truck.

Smiths and Lacourses and Grohalskis run from other houses to the truck.

I'm the last one there.

They haul out the driver, a big man all shaken up, face crumpled, blood around his mouth. They say, "He can walk! He's okay. Stand back, stand back. There might be fire."

He was hauling crates of bottles, and there's glass all over the road.

That shriek I heard as the truck went over . . . I mud-skate around to the back and look in.

Something red wiggles, heaves, and struggles way in the back, up against the cab. It raises its head and shrieks again, and I know what it is.

Jet knows, too. Back in the Taylor yard, he neighs.

I, Alice Brown, am a little shy. Dad calls me Scaredy. Grandma calls me Quiet. I do not walk up to strangers and speak to them.

Never mind that. I, Alice Brown, skate back to the driver and grab his sleeve. "Mister," I say to his bloody mouth and teary eyes, "you've got a pony in the back."

He mutters. He spits, wipes his mouth on the other sleeve, and nods. "Yeah," he says past a knocked-out tooth. "Haulin' it for a frien'." He does not ask how the pony is, much less struggle around to the back and look.

I skate back around the truck. People are sweeping up glass. "Careful," they say. "Don't go in there."

"There's a pony in there."

They know that. The pony shrieks and Jet answers. "Wait till we sweep, kid. Wait till we know this truck won't explode."

At last I'm in the truck, beside the pony. Her golden eyes roll wildly. She struggles to get up, but the rope twisted under her holds her down.

People climb in here with me. A knife cuts the rope and the pony lurches up. Scared wild, she's all set to gallop out of here through glass and people. I catch her rough rope halter and hang on.

Jinny's got the other side of the halter. Together we ease the pony down onto the road. She bucks and plunges, but we hold on. Jinny says, "She doesn't look hurt." And she doesn't. She looks terrified and battered, but not even her slender legs seem injured.

The driver plods up beside us. Someone asks him, "What about this?" meaning the pony. He looks at me. "You got shomeplace t' keep it?" His missing tooth makes talking hard.

Of course I haven't any place to put her, but I nod eagerly. Jinny nods, too.

He mouths, "Okay. Keep it."

"Keep it? You mean for always?"

He nods. "Dog meat," he explains. "Jush dog meat. Keep it." He turns away.

Jinny says very softly—I've never heard her speak so softly—"You got yourself a pony."

Between us we lead her out of the crowd and the glass.

Jinny says, "Wait." She struggles back to the truck while I hold my pony fast.

Her coat is red with white tips, like spilled salt. Her white mane and tail haven't been brushed in years. She's maybe two-thirds Jet's size—the perfect size for me. She shudders and shivers and snaps at my hand, but I hold on fast.

Jinny comes back with the rope from the truck. "You can't ride her home, she's too shook up."

So am I.

"We'll tie her behind Jet and walk her home. Let's go."

Yes, let's go! Before the driver changes his mind or someone calls the dog meat people.

We borrow more rope from the Taylors. We tie one end around Jet's middle and the other end to my pony's rope halter. Meanwhile the ponies squeal like pigs and push their foreheads together. Jinny says, "They like each other." I hope that's what the squealing means.

Four o'clock on Jinny's watch and we're climbing O'Neal Road. Jinny and I ride Jet. My pony trails behind on her rope lead. She still trembles and shudders now and then, but she follows Jet almost meekly. "Good thing he's here," Jinny says. "We'd have a heck of a time with her without him!"

I keep glancing back to make sure my pony's still there.

The road is washed out, all mud and rocks. Jet walks carefully, steadily. My pony stumbles along, her small hoofs scraping and sliding.

I have a pony. I led this pony out of a truck that overturned on mud. If the truck had gone slower . . . if the rain hadn't roared down like Niagara Falls . . . if some idiot hadn't sent my pony to the dog meat people, I wouldn't have her. Grandma would call my having her a Miracle.

Grandma. Honolulu! I lean to breathe in Jinny's ear, "I can't take this pony home."

"No kidding!"

"Where am I taking her?"

"Where do you think, Brainless? To our barn."

That's certainly what I had hoped! "You sure your folks won't mind?"

Jinny shrugs. "There's Cow and Speckles Calf now, and Jack's rabbits and Jerry's ducks and Jan's skunk, and Jet. What's a new pony more or less?"

"What about hay?"

"Won't need any till winter."

I'll have time to solve that problem.

We climb higher. Below us the soaked roofs of Granton gleam in near sunshine. Along the road soaked Indian paints and daisies almost lift their heads.

"Jinny, my dad mustn't know about her."

"Bingo."

"She's a secret forever."

"What're you going to call her?"

Jet pauses to blow and pant on the steepest stretch of road. Both of us turn around to look at my pony.

"I could call her Salt. See the white tips in her coat?"

Jinny says, "Mmmm."

"Ginger?"

"Lots of Gingers."

Actually, I used to daydream about an elegant pony named Princess. But the way my real miracle pony tosses her tangled mane and the funny light in her eyes warn me that Princess is not her name.

"Why don't I call her Miracle, 'cause that's what she is?"

Jinny snorts.

"Or . . . Lucky."

I wonder what her "real" name is, or was. Wonder if she ever had one. Wonder if any kid ever rode or brushed or petted her. I'll never know.

"Lucky . . . ," says Jinny, trying it out.

"Lucky," I say firmly.

"Bingo," Jinny agrees. "She's pretty, you know that?"

"Pretty?" My Lucky has four legs, a mane and tail, and lively eyes. And she's mine. But pretty?

"Brush her up. Let her graze. You'll see."

Jet shifts weight and swishes tail, ready to climb. We turn forward.

"Jinny, look! A rainbow!"

A wide, soft rainbow arches up over O'Neal farm on the hilltop and comes down by Rocky Rise, behind our house.

Jinny breathes out. "Holy Honolulu!"

Grandma would say, "That's a sign."

I feel she would be right. It's a sign for Lucky and me and our new life together.

Grandma loves rainbows. I hope she's out on the back porch watching this one. That way, she won't see us pass by.

* * * * * * * * * * * * * **2**

It sure beats me how calm I feel!
Here I've taken on a living, breathing pony for whom I haven't a roof or a hay seed. I don't know if she's even trained to ride. I might have to train her myself. As though I had an idea how to do that! I don't think even Jinny knows how.

But I'm not scared at all. Setting the table, my hands don't shake. I haven't dropped a glass. I feel perfectly sure that I can and will do whatever Lucky needs me to do. I don't know where that feeling comes from, but it's like a bright, steady rainbow inside me.

Jinny and I turned the two ponies loose together in Back Field, behind her house. Back Field is sort of fenced-in with old leaning posts, wire, and stone walls. Grandpa O'Neal grazed a herd of Jersey cows there once. Now that his son, Mr. O'Neal, works down in Granton like everyone else, fence posts have fallen. Wire's been cut to use someplace else. Stone walls have crumbled. But it's a big field. Jet stays in here pretty well with Cow and Speckles Calf, and Jinny says Lucky will stay here with Jet. I'm betting she's right.

Jinny went off to help her brothers with chores.

I leaned on the gate and watched Lucky.

She stayed right close to Jet. They nickered and pranced a bit. Jet was like a kid with a new puppy. He trotted, and Lucky trotted around him. He stopped, and Lucky ran in to nuzzle him. Big, black Jet and ragged, red Lucky stood close together shaking manes, whisking tails, and muttering. Then they got down to grazing, black and white tails swishing side by side. Neither of them looked my way. They had each other.

I still didn't really believe that this miracle had happened and Lucky was mine. But as I watched her graze, hungry and happy, I began to believe it and I began to think about what she would need.

She needed brushing. (Jinny had brushes.)

She needed rich pasture (which stretched all around her).

She needed exercise.

Come morning, I would climb on her back.

The amazing thought came to me quietly, gently. I would climb on Lucky's back, and I wouldn't be scared. Inside me this bright, steady rainbow arched and shone. Lucky and I belonged together, and everything would be okay.

I called to her, "See you tomorrow, Lucky!"

Lucky threw up her head and shied. Jet looked at me, twitched his ears, and moved between us.

I could have leaned on the gate and watched them till dark. But I knew Grandma was looking out for me and Dad would be home soon. I dragged myself away.

Now, while I set the table, Grandma hums a hymn, "Crown Him with Many Crowns," and stirs Irish stew. Evening light slants in the back window and sparkles on plates, glass, and embroidery.

Grandma embroidered a rose garden on the tablecloth. She embroidered cats climbing vines on the curtains. She embroidered every curtain, bedspread, and bureau scarf in the house with tall, strong flowers for Dad, horses for me, and cats for herself.

I lay the third fork and pull back the curtain to look out. From here I see a tall lilac hedge between the house and Old Pasture. There's a ragged gap in the hedge so we can get to an old tool shed behind it. If Dad didn't have his NO ANIMALS rule, Lucky could live there. Across Old Pasture, Rocky Rise cuts off the sunset.

"Alice, what are you staring at?"

"Oh, nothing much." I drop the curtain.

"You know it's Friday?"

"Um?"

"You set the weekday china! What are you thinking about?"

I wish I could tell her! She would be so happy for me. But she couldn't, or wouldn't, keep Lucky secret from Dad.

On Fridays we celebrate the end of Dad's work week with special china and his favorite Irish stew and a rainbow-embroidered tablecloth. Grandma whisks away the rose garden and spreads the rainbow. As we take out the old china she says, "I bet I know what's bothering you. It's B and T, isn't it?"

B and T—Bones and Tubs—are Jinny's and my enemies. They're big boys from Granton. Every now and then they sneak up the hill to make us miserable.

For once I haven't been thinking about B and T! Since meeting Lucky I haven't given them a thought, but they'll do just fine to cover up my secret.

"I've been thinking what Jinny and I can do to make them back off."

"Say what?"

Louder. "What can we do to make them quit bothering us?"

Grandma sets out shining glasses. "When I was young, there was this older girl in school kept bothering me."

"Older? In a different class?"

"We were all together. One-room school, you know."

Once Grandma showed me that one-room schoolhouse, on the other side of Granton. Now it's someone's home.

"Promised land!" she says, pausing to remember. "How that girl bothered me! She laughed if I dropped my chalk. She tittered if I walked across the room. As for my clothes . . ."

I see real, old hurt in Grandma's face.

But now she brightens. "I cooked her goose!"

"How, Grandma?"

Grandma starts to waltz around the table, rubbing her hands happily. "That girl had a weakness, and a mean boy found it out. He put a snake in her desk."

"Holy Honolulu!"

"Nothing serious. Just a little garden snake, this long." Grandma holds her hands a yard apart. "So when she opened the desk, up rose this snake." Grandma's hands slither upward, wiggling.

"This girl screamed. I mean, screamed. Then all the girls screamed. The boys roared for joy. The teacher jumped up on her desk. She had a weakness, too.

"Me, I walked over there and picked up the snake. Poor thing, he didn't know what was going on. I turned him loose outside."

I can just see pint-size Grandma marching through a crowd of roaring boys with a snake in her small hands.

But I don't see how it cooked that girl's goose.

"Is that all?" I ask her.

"Is that all? Let me tell you, that girl never

laughed at me again, not even when I told a joke! After that she had to respect me. That's what you have to do—teach B and T respect."

Right. But B and T have no weakness with snakes or anything else.

"Tell you one thing we could do right now, tonight, that would help."

Grandma trips over to the dresser where she keeps her magazines. She pokes an ad under my nose. "We could cut your hair, like this. This here style would suit you much better than that dusty ponytail. B and T would know you were somebody."

The ad shows a girl, older and thinner than I, standing in front of a Honda. It's advertising the Honda, not the girl, but Grandma points to her sleek, short hair.

"See, she's got your same heart-shaped face. See how smart she looks? Neat as a Siamese cat. That ponytail style suits your pal Jinny fine, but it doesn't do a thing for you."

Grandma's right. Skinny Jinny needs a weight of hair so she won't blow away. I don't need it.

Grandma sees me hesitate. "We could do it right after supper."

"I like it, Grandma. It's pretty." It would make me look almost pretty.

"My heavens, let's do it!"

"But not right now." Jinny likes me to follow her lead. I don't want to cut my hair different from hers, especially now when she's helping me with Lucky.

Grandma sighs. Actually, this is not our first discussion about my hairdo.

"I'll keep the scissors handy."

The front screen door opens and shuts. Tired feet pad down the hall toward the kitchen.

I look to the door to warn Grandma that Dad is coming. She has not heard the door or his steps. He walks in suddenly and she shies like a startled pony.

He pats her shoulder. "Are my girls happy?"

Dad looks like a tired soap opera star—tall, dark, and craggy. He hugs Grandma's shoulder and looks at me kindly, the way Jet does, but he does not smile. He almost never smiles.

Grandma recovers her dignity. "Your girls," she snaps, "are hungry. I hope you are, Dave."

"Do I smell Irish stew?"

"Is this Friday?"

"I'm starved."

Dad goes to wash his hands at the sink. He

says loudly over his shoulder, "Got to go in Saturday. Special order."

I'm glad his back is turned so he doesn't see my face light up.

Saturdays, Dad likes to work around the place. He likes to mow and rake and pick up. He especially likes to work on his flower beds by the front gate, where his tall, tough flowers stand up straight. He plants goldenrod as a flower, though most people call it a weed. He plants gladioli (which means "swords") and tall phlox and tiger lilies and hollyhocks. These get weeded on Saturday, and I'm supposed to help.

But if Dad takes off tomorrow at dawn to do a special order, I bet I can run right up the hill to Lucky. Secretly.

* * * * * * * * * * * * **3**

*H*ow come I'm so calm?

Through swirling mist I watch Lucky and Jet. They trot across Back Field close together, jostling and whisking tails. They circle and pause, forehead to forehead. Silver mist drifts slowly around them as I watch from the gate.

That excited red pony playing out there is mine. I didn't dream her. She's real. She eats grass and breathes air. Her small hoofs scar the earth. Some of that fresh, steaming dung on the ground is hers.

I'm getting ready to slide a bit between her

teeth and climb aboard. After that . . . well, anything might happen.

So why doesn't my breath wheeze and my heart pound?

Because when I look at Lucky this soft, bright rainbow shines inside me. I know I can do whatever needs doing.

Here comes Jinny from the barn, jeans full of carrots, swinging two bridles. Calmly I take the ancient, frayed bridle she holds out. It's warm, soft, and greasy, looks like it'll crumble at a touch. Looks like Jinny's Grandpa used it. I bet he did.

Jinny opens the gate, and we go in.

This is it. I feel like I'm walking through a dream.

Back Field is short-cropped grass dotted with purple clover patches and orange Indian paints. Robins tug at earthworms. An oriole and a catbird sing from line maples along the stone wall. Out in the mist the two ponies pause in their play and turn toward us, ears pricked, nostrils wide. I reach in and draw two carrots out of Jinny's back pocket.

Jinny whistles to Jet.

Jet wiggles ears and shakes mane.

Lucky shies.

Jinny whistles again.

Lucky flings herself high and sideways. She comes down galloping.

"Hey, Jinny, quit the whistling! It spooks her."

"No kidding!"

Jet plods toward us.

Lucky pounds away to the far side of the field and turns to face us.

Jinny sighs. "We'll have a time to catch her now. And I've just got an hour. Then I have to do chores with Jack and Jerry."

"Me, too." I have no chores with Jinny's rough brothers, praise be! But Grandma wants me back home to vacuum.

Jet arrives and nuzzles Jinny for his carrot. She pays him, then slides her bit into his mouth. "Come on, Alice, climb on. You can't catch your miracle on foot, but Jet can. Maybe."

We spend most of our free hour trotting around Back Field after Lucky. At first I can see she's really spooked. When we get close her legs tremble and the whites of her eyes flash. But slowly it turns into a game. Lucky pauses to graze, watching us from one bright eye. As we close in she tosses her mane, snorts, and gallops off.

"Honolulu!" Jinny says at last. "This is work! Take five."

We slide down off Jet and sit on the stone wall. Jinny holds on to Jet's reins. He stands patiently, settling his weight to one side. Out in the field Lucky twitches her ears at us.

I get an idea. "Maybe . . . maybe she'll come to us now."

"Hmmm," says Jinny. "Looks like she might be thinking about it."

Lucky's ears twitch forward. She blows. Jet blows.

Jinny breathes, "Hey . . ."

Step by slow step, Lucky comes to us. She pushes her forehead against Jet's forehead, sighs, and settles. The game is over.

Jinny murmurs, "Show her the carrot."

I hold my carrot like a candle. Slowly I stand up and step toward the ponies. "Looky, Lucky," I say softly. "Looky, Lucky."

Lucky's nostrils quiver.

I open my palm flat around the carrot, and that's a good thing. Lucky's yellow teeth snap up the carrot before I see it go.

While her teeth crunch I grab the rope halter. Lucky is mine. Jinny grabs the other side of the halter.

Grandma has a saying, She who hesitates is lost. I do not hesitate. I slide my thumb right in where I know there shouldn't be teeth. The bit goes in. I pull the headpiece over the stiff-pricked ears, and we're there. Here. Home.

Jinny says softly, "Bingo."

I look into Lucky's near eye. A warning light goes on, but no panic. She's been bridled before, somewhere, sometime.

She who hesitates . . . I grab Lucky's wild, coarse mane and scramble up her side.

Singing toads, I wish I'd brushed her first! I'll never get all this red horsehair off my jeans!

I settle on her back and gather the ancient reins. Now, if only the bridle doesn't fall into dust . . .

Jinny warns, "I'm letting go."

"Just don't whistle."

Jinny lets go.

Lucky snorts and half rears.

I clamp knees, tighten reins. The bridle holds.

Lucky stamps in a tight circle left.

I draw on the right rein.

We stand.

I feel Lucky decide, This is okay. I can live with it.

I remember the warning light in her eye and don't relax. I sit tight with tight reins. Sunshine breaks through mist.

I wake up from a sort-of dream. Robins, orioles, and blackbirds sing. I smell Lucky's warm sweat. Gripping the reins in one hand, I pat her damp neck with the other. "Looky, Lucky," I tell her gently, "we're okay."

And sunshine spreads over Back Field, over Lucky and me.

* * * * * * * * * * * * 4

P romised land!" Grandma marvels. "Look at this horsehair on your jeans!"

"Ah. Um. We've been riding a lot."

"Here, brush it off before it murders the machine." Grandma hands me a stiff cleaning brush and spreads a newspaper at my feet. Red, white-tipped horsehair rains onto the newspaper. Grandma hums the hymn "Behold a Stranger at the Door" while she loads Dad's work clothes and a cup of Last Chance into the machine. Then she says, "The O'Neal horse is black."

"That's why they call him Jet."

29

"What say? Oh, Jet. Jet black. Yes. Well, how come this hair is red as Jinny O'Neal's?"

I mumble to the newspaper, "They've got a new pony up at the farm."

"What say?"

Louder. "There's a new pony. Her name is Lucky."

"Does this new pony have anything to do with the accident at Taylors'?"

Grandma doesn't miss much! She reads the paper, watches local news, and gossips at the Granton Senior Center. Actually, this is sort of a relief. I don't have to keep the whole story secret, just the fact that Lucky is mine.

"Yes, it does. She was in the truck that turned over. The driver didn't know what to do with her."

"So he sold her cheap?"

"Ah . . . actually, he gave her away."

"My heavens!"

"He was only taking her for dog meat."

Grandma steps back. Shakes her head. Briefly, she looks as shocked as I feel. "I see," she says. "That's why she's called Lucky. She was lucky Jinny O'Neal was there."

"Mmmmm . . ."

"And you were lucky, too." Grandma points

at the filthy jeans I still hold. "Sure looks like you ride her!"

"Oh, yes. Yes, I do. Now there's two ponies, we each ride one. And I brush her, too, Grandma."

"You work on her?"

"You wouldn't believe how neat she is now. Like a short-haired cat. This won't happen again, Grandma." At least, not till Lucky gets her winter coat.

Grandma takes the jeans and brush. "Running around at O'Neals' is downright rough on your clothes, Alice. I didn't say much about that T-shirt, but . . ."

Two weeks ago Jinny laughed at my T-shirt. Grandma had embroidered a tricolored kitten on the shoulder. Jinny made fun: "A Taylor toddler would look cute in that shirt!"

Anger heated me like fever. Anger at Grandma for embroidering a cute kitten. Anger at me for letting Jinny see it.

Trudging home alone down O'Neal Road, I stepped off behind a briar patch. First I looked carefully all around. It was about time for B and T to turn up and torment us. They might be hiding up a tree or in shadow. But I saw only the hot, empty road and briars. I heard only catbirds and mosquitoes.

I yanked that T-shirt off and raked it seven swipes through the briars. I hurled it to the ground and jumped on it seven times. Satisfied, I hauled it back on—with a shudder—and came on home.

Now I say, "You were real nice about that T-shirt, Grandma."

"Promised land, I'll say so! But this is the second disaster in two weeks. Try not to wreck your clothes like a little Taylor wrecks toys. They cost too much."

Grandma stuffs the jeans in the machine and flicks the switch. "And work on that horse, that Lucky. Brush her better."

* * * * * * * * * * * * * **5**

July 16
8 A.M.

*J*inny rides Jet down the driveway past the barn. Lucky follows Jet like his shadow. I hardly have to hold the reins.

Little Jan O'Neal stands in the driveway with his pet skunk, Kitty, on his shoulder.

Kitty was a baby last spring when his mother was hit by a car, and Jan saved him off the road. Now he's getting big.

Jinny says Jan is not bright, but he's great with animals. He smiles his strangely sweet smile at us as we ride past.

I call to Jinny's back, "Kitty sure has grown!"

She calls back, "We're trying to get rid of

him, send him back to the woods. But he keeps coming home."

"My dad says animals raised tame can't make it in the woods."

"A skunk can. See, he'll eat anything. And if he's got his stinker he can defend himself. We didn't fix Kitty's stinker like Mom wanted, so he'll do fine."

With no sign from Jinny, Jet turns down the dirt road. Lucky follows like Mary's lamb.

"Doesn't Kitty stink up your barn?"

"Never needed to. Never been scared. But we're getting sick of tiptoeing around, just in case."

We always take the ponies out of Back Field this way, by the driveway and down the road. We could ride out of several fence-gaps, but we don't want the ponies to notice those gaps. They know to turn down the road and turn again onto Orchard Track, and walk through the old apple orchard to the edge of the hay mowing.

From here we can ride anywhere on the Hill. We can turn right to Blueberry Lot or cross the mowing to Sugar Bush. We can turn left to Old Pasture, all rocks and Indian paints and daisies. These lots are all divided, lined off from one another by stone walls and "line" trees, great old maples and some elms. Then, down to the left of Old Pasture, Rocky Rise tilts steeply into the sky. We like to race up Rocky Rise, stand there in the sky, and look down on my house and O'Neal Road and Granton way below.

All this is ours to ride in, race, and pick berries in.

All this is ours—and B and T's.

Blue sky shines through the dark old apple trees. We draw rein on the edge of the mowing.

The O'Neals still harvest this hay. The long, thick grass here is a crop. We're supposed to stay in the middle track and not trample the hay. But we have seen crushed grass, paths through the mowing, that B and T might have made.

We pause in the shade of the oldest, biggest apple tree and spy out the field.

"Nothing moving," Jinny mutters.

Jet nods and paws earth. To Jet, the middle track leading through the hay means, Race! He wants to start.

I murmur, "Listen."

Lucky shifts weight and swishes tail.

A hawk screams, high up. Mosquitoes buzz, moving in on us. A cuckoo calls.

Jinny tosses her ponytail. "Let's go." She clucks to Jet and rides out onto the track.

Lucky prances after.

Jinny shouts, "Race!" And leans forward.

Actually, this is not really fair. Jinny's ahead to start with, and the track is narrow. But we're used to it. We don't really mind.

Jinny yells, "Yaaaah, Jet!" They take off.

I yell, "Yaaah, Lucky!" But Lucky has already taken off.

Small hoofs thunder. Wind slaps my face and lifts my heavy hair. Far-off line trees gallop toward us.

Jinny lets out a whoop of joy.

Then Jinny whistles.

Before I can say, "Blast off!" Lucky soars high off the track into tall grass.

I grab her mane.

Lucky lands hard. She bucks, rears, paws the air.

I slide down her tail.

Lucky rushes off.

I hurt. I sit on hard ground in deep grass and listen to Lucky's hoofs pound farther and farther away, into silence.

Jet's steady hoofbeats thud nearby and stop.

Jinny comes pushing through the grass to me. "Sorry," she says briskly. "I forgot."

Hurting, I look up at her.

"I forgot!"

"Sure you did."

"You think I spooked Lucky on purpose?"

I think this is the first time I have ever actually been mad at Jinny.

"You wanted to win."

"Blast off! I was winning anyhow."

"Because we couldn't get by you. Like every time."

"Alice, get up."

"Maybe I can't get up. Maybe my back's broken."

"Holy Honolulu, Alice, come on!" Jinny reaches me a helping hand.

I grab it, yank, and haul her down in the grass with me. We wrestle, roll, and pant. Then we lie back, all dirty, and laugh.

"Jinny, your hair's all hay-seed!"

"You should see yours! Hey!" Jinny freezes up. She whispers, "What was that?"

"What?" I'm still laughing.

"Shhhh!"

I stop laughing.

Jinny rises on an elbow. Her lean face tenses and whitens so the freckles stand out like golden sand.

Not far away a voice speaks.

It's an almost-man voice, deep, with cracks. It says, "They ran off about here."

My eyes meet Jinny's. She nods, and her lips form the words "B and T."

Our enemies. The sneaky spies who watch us from trees and shadows and pull mean tricks. The dangerous aliens. They're here.

One time they rigged a cord across O'Neal Road to trip Jet. He stumbled. We rolled off over his head, and they ran off laughing.

One time they stole our lunch. We had left our sandwiches on a rock while we picked wild strawberries. When we came back our lunches were gone. It had to be B and T.

One time Jinny was walking up O'Neal Road alone, and they jumped her, whooping and waving sticks. She ran off through the briars with B and T on her heels, whipping their sticks in the air, swish! crack! She managed to lose them in the orchard. Later she told me, "If only you had been there, Alice, we could have lasered them away." That gave me a good, warm feeling. But I'm not sure it's true. B and

T together are stronger than the two of us together.

Here come B and T now. I gather myself to rise and run.

Jinny grabs my wrist. "Stay down."

She's right. The long grass will hide us if B and T don't follow our trails.

A squeaky voice shrills, "There's the black horse!" Jet waits near us. I wish he was trained so we could signal him to move off!

Deeper Voice says, "All by himself. I bet those horses just busted themselves loose. The kids aren't here."

Squeaker, "Tell you what. Let's us steal the horses."

Deeper Voice, "You ride?"

"Yeah, I can ride, but we don't have to. Just catch 'em and lead 'em."

Deeper Voice, "To where?"

Squeaker, "Anywhere. Hold 'em for ransom."

Deeper Voice, "Ransom? Those kids don't have money!"

Squeaker, "Don't have to be money at all. Listen . . ."

I listen with my ears twitching like Lucky's, but the voices move off, mumbling.

Now I see Jet's back over the high grass.

Grazing, he wanders nearer. Earth rumbles slightly as Lucky comes trotting back to him.

Jinny murmurs, "The aliens have gone."

I start to rise.

"Wait! Might be a trick."

We lie still a while longer. Lucky and Jet whicker and nicker nearby. Hoofs thud as they play happily through the O'Neal hay crop.

Jinny kneels up and parts the grass tops, looking out. "I thought they'd follow our tracks. Wouldn't you follow clear tracks like ours?"

"They didn't think we were here. They thought the ponies had busted themselves loose."

"Yeah, that's what they said. Dunno. You'd think they would have seen us, riding."

"Must have come just too late for that. Praise be!"

"Well, they've gone to hatch some Evil Plan to steal the ponies." Jinny brushes dirt from her hair and clothes, and stands up. "Alice, we need an Evil Plan of our own. Quick."

* * * * * * * * * * * * * **6**

So, Dad, what would you do?"

A long time ago Dad was a boy. He'll know what B and T are really likely to do and what we should do.

He lies in the back porch hammock, beer can in hand, watching fireflies. They wink on and off like Christmas lights in the dark hedge. Every year Dad mourns that there are fewer fireflies and growls about pollution. But it seems to me there's no end to them. If they all winked on at once you could read by their light. But they take turns. Dad says they've got a winking code that tells if they are male or female, and which kind of firefly they are.

Dad loves fireflies and tall, tough flowers. I'm not always sure he loves me.

Now I sit on the back porch steps to tell him this story and ask his advice. And he sighs.

He doesn't want to talk. I know he wants to drink his beer in peace and watch fireflies and think to himself. But Honolulu! There's no time when Dad does want to talk. Though Grandma says when I was little, before Mom died, he used to talk and laugh a lot.

Slowly, heavily, he says, "Let me get this perfectly straight. You and this Jennifer—"

"Jinny."

"You are riding through O'Neals' Mowing and got thrown."

"I got thrown. I was riding Lucky, my—the new pony. Jinny whistled and spooked her."

"You were down there in the grass, hidden. How did . . . Jane get down there with you?"

"Jinny. She came back to me, and I pulled her down."

Dad takes this in. "Aha. You stood up for yourself."

"Kind of. I was kind of in orbit about her whistling. But it was an accident. She forgot."

"Sure. Oh, sure. So now you're both down there hidden, and these kids come along."

"B and T."

"Bones and Tubs. And they plan, at the top of their voices, to steal the horses."

"That's it."

Dad takes a last swig and sets the beer can under the hammock.

"Who are these Bones and Tubs, anyhow? Where do they come from?"

"We don't know their names. We call them that because that's how they look. They come up from Granton just to pester us."

"Pester you how?"

I tell about the stolen sandwiches, the cord across the road, and even the sticks, though that story is sort of embarrassing.

Dad swings the hammock slowly. "Hmmm. Sounds like you can't call the cops on them, even about that business tripping the horse. You might have got hurt, for sure. But you can't prove they did it."

"Dad, they might really steal those ponies."

Dad sighs. "Stealing ponies takes more effort, more planning than those bozos want to put out. You ask me, Alice, I'd say they just want you to worry and fret."

This is interesting. "You don't think they meant it?"

Dad answers with a question. "Why do you think they didn't follow your tracks in the crushed grass?"

"We figure they thought the ponies were loose by themselves. They didn't know we were there."

"Hah! If they've got the sense they were born with they knew you were there, at the end of those tracks. They talked loud so you'd be sure to hear them, and worry and fret. That's what I would do if I were them! I'd shout my Evil Plan. Then I'd laugh all the way home and forget it. That's what I think, Alice. If I were you I'd lose no sleep over it."

For a while Dad is silent, watching fireflies. Then he says, "But I do lose sleep over you, Alice."

That startles me. I turn to look at him closely. By firefly light and the light from Grandma's window I see him as a dark form swinging very gently, one sneaker pushing the floor. He says, "I worry that you need muscle."

"Muscle?"

"You remind me more of a morning glory vine than an upstanding hollyhock."

Vine? Hollyhock? Since when are we discussing flowers?

"I'm glad you stood up for yourself with Janet."

What was it with Dad and that name? "Jinny, Dad."

"But you need to do more of that."

Strangely, I'm thinking of the new rainbow that shines in me when I'm with Lucky. Too bad Dad can't see either one—Lucky or my rainbow.

He says softly, "I wish your mother was with us. She would know what's good for you. I'm not sure I do."

Maybe Dad doesn't know what's good for me, but I do. Lucky is good for me.

I shut my eyes and think hot sunlight, Indian paints and daisies, and Lucky under me. She lends me her muscle, her strong speed and fun. We gallop across Old Pasture and up Rocky Rise. In this daydream it's just us. I don't know where Jinny and Jet are, but they're not in front of us.

At the top of Rocky Rise we stand and look down on this house and Granton below. Lucky paws and whisks her tail, and I tell her, "Okay. Yaaah, Lucky."

Then we canter along Rocky Rise, with only wispy clouds between us and the sun.

* * * * * * * * * * * * **7**

July 19

1 *P.M.*

The Great Evil Plan comes to me as I sit here alone in my new secret place.

It's the world's best plan. Cosmic. I can almost see the horror and shock on B and T's faces. Will they ever be sorry!

Here in my secret place I grin and hug myself with delight.

Early this morning I crunched up the O'Neal driveway. Dishes clashed in the house. Jinny was washing up.

Jan and Kitty were playing by the barn with a tricolored kitten Grandma would die for. That is, Jan and the kitten played. Kitty sat by looking annoyed. Actually, Kitty looked like Dad when he doesn't want to talk.

I told Jan, "I'll just go in the barn and get my—the bridle."

Jan just smiled.

In the big, dim old barn I lifted the bridle off its hook and took a carrot from the bin. Then a new idea hit me. I stood very still and thought it out.

As I came out of the barn Kitty stood up and danced. He stomped slowly from one front paw to the other, back and forth, beady eyes on the tricolored kitten. His striped tail stiffened and rose up. Kitty was decidedly annoyed.

Quickly I skipped across the driveway. Dad had told me all about that skunk dance and what it means.

Very calm, Jan spoke. I had never heard him speak before. He doesn't talk with people. But to Kitty he said quite distinctly, "No. No, Kitty." Then he stooped and scooped Kitty up his arms.

I squeezed my eyes shut and pinched my nose.

When I dared to peek, Jan was walking back into the barn with Kitty on his shoulder. The tricolored kitten bounded alongside.

That must have been when the Great Evil

Plan came to me. That moment. But at the time I was too full of my other New Idea to think about it.

All alone, all by myself, I came to Back Field gate swinging the bridle.

My New Idea was, I COULD RIDE ALL ALONE, ALL BY MYSELF.

Why not?

I could ride off on Lucky and take my own way before Jinny finished washing dishes. We could meet later in Mowing or Orchard or Pasture.

Why not?

Thrilled—and a bit uneasy—I moved toward the ponies. Lucky neighed hello. Jet looked up from grazing.

The idea of riding out into open space with no Jinny leading was thrilling. But suppose, just suppose I met B and T alone, all by myself! We hadn't seen them since that time in the Mowing. Pretty soon they should be moving in on us again to spy and jump and chase.

That thought slowed me down, but it didn't stop me. I wanted so awfully to see the sky up ahead instead of Jinny's back!

When I was close to the ponies I drew the

carrot from my pocket and called, "Looky, Lucky!" as she expected me to call.

I did not expect both ponies to trot right up to me eyeing the same carrot! I had to drop the bridle, snap the carrot in half, and hold each half out on a flat palm.

Lucky snatched her half, and I snatched her halter. Now she wears a "new" soft O'Neal halter, instead of the rough rope halter she came with.

Moments later I rode off, alone by myself with Lucky. She nickered for Jet to come. I hadn't thought of that, and for a second I almost worried. But Jet stayed put, looking after us in a puzzled way. Next time I glanced back he was grazing.

Lucky was as used to following Jet as I was used to following Jinny. She kept shrilling for Jet and trying to circle back. I had to grip the reins right smart and give the orders.

Where to? I didn't want to ride right down the driveway past Jinny at the window. She might be annoyed.

Nudging and kicking and sawing reins, I got Lucky to the far end of Back Field. A stone wall lay crumbled there under pink wild roses.

Carefully we stepped through stones and roses into Blueberry Lot.

Out of sight and smell of Jet, I relaxed the reins. Right off, Lucky went to prance and side-step, toss and whisk. We danced up the center aisle between blueberry rows.

What about B and T? Any bush might hide them. Dad might not think them very danger-ous, but I didn't want to meet them alone.

I pulled up. Lucky pawed and shook her mane while I pricked my ears, listening.

Distant crows and jays called. Flies homed in on horse scent, but no voices squeaked or muttered or whispered. No shadows sneaked behind bushes.

Maybe it was too early for B and T. They might even have other things to do besides make us miserable.

Inside me, a soft, bright rainbow glowed and spread.

I loosed the reins. "Okay. Yaaah, Lucky!"

Lucky took off.

We played all morning, just us. We really got to know each other and move right together. I learned how bright and fun Lucky is. She's tricky but not mean. I hope she thinks the same of me!

Just about hot noontime I slid down off Lucky to rest on a stone wall between Old Pasture and Wood Lot. A giant line maple leaned over the wall, and Lucky went to graze in its shade. I left her loose. I figured if she ran off, she'd just go back to Jet.

I pulled a little Coke can out of my shirt pocket. As I tipped my head back to drink I noticed this huge shadow just above me in the maple.

A rotty, tilting, falling-down tree house rested across three maple branches. It looked older than the Bible, but the rope ladder dangling down the trunk looked good, almost new.

I'm sitting in the tree house now, cool among the leaves, looking out the door. Old Pasture stretches away to Rocky Rise. It's carpeted with clover and paints and daisies like a wide earth rainbow. White and gray rocks sprinkled with mica gleam here and there.

This is a great place to be alone! Dad would like to be alone here.

I bet Jinny doesn't know about this tree house. If she'd known it she would have shown it to me.

I bet nobody in the world knows about this ancient tree house but me. Like Lucky's bridle, it's ready to fall apart. I shift my weight carefully on the rotting floor. Good thing I'm not scared of spiders. Their webs hang off the walls like tapestries. And here's a sticky bit of . . . chewing gum? by my hand. Wonder how old that is! I scrape it off the floor with my fingernails and drop it out the door. Ick.

Chewing gum reminds me of B and T. I've seen them pop gum while they sneer at us.

Thinking of B and T reminds me of . . .

I sit bolt upright. The floor creaks as I move.

Thinking of B and T reminds me of the Great Evil Plan I didn't know I had!

It must have been hatching in my head all morning since Kitty danced, and I was too busy playing with Lucky to see it.

Jinny said we needed an Evil Plan of our own. Here it is, full-fledged and grinning. Here it is, muscular, brilliant, wicked!

I, Alice Brown, alone by myself, with no help from Jinny, know how to teach respect to B and T!

8

July 19
2 P.M.

I ride slowly across Old Pasture. Heat seems to bounce off rocks and hang in the air. Sweat slicks Lucky's coat.

As soon as the Great Evil Plan hit me I shinnied down the rope, climbed on Lucky, and set out. Jinny's got to hear this plan!

But wait. Hold on. I pull the reins back. Lucky is glad to stop. She stands panting, head low. Far away, something moves through heat-shimmers. It walks slowly, like us, toward the Wood Lot. Is it B and T?

Like an Indian scout in an old picture I shade my eyes with my hand.

It's Jinny on Jet.

"Yaaah, Lucky!" I loosen the reins, lean forward, and nudge.

Lucky blows and shakes her mane.

"See Jet? Go for Jet. Yaaah!"

Lucky takes a slow, unwilling step.

Jinny and Jet almost reach the Wood Lot. In a moment they'll be out of sight in the trees. I yell, "Yaaah, Jinny!"

They stop. Jet neighs.

Lucky pricks her ears and rises to a trot.

Jinny and Jet just stand there, waiting. Why don't they come to meet us?

"Jinny!" I shout. "Something wrong?"

No answer.

Blast off! She's in orbit because I rode off alone this morning. I'm lucky she waits for me at all.

Trotting close, I see Jinny's unsmiling face, Jet's patient face, and a third face. This one is small and black and white. It peers at us over Jinny's elbow.

So that's why they wait so still and silent! Panting, we pull up at a pretty safe distance. "Jinny, what are you doing with Kitty?"

Very softly, Jinny says, "Losing him in the Wood Lot, I hope."

"Holy Honolulu, I'm just in time!"

Softly, "Want to come?"

"Don't lose Kitty, Jinny!"

Gently, "Talk softer. He's got his stinker. He can take care of—"

"We need him!"

Politely, "Alice, talk softer."

"We need him for the Great Evil Plan! I just thought of it."

Sweetly, "If you don't shut your mouth, Kitty will shut it."

She's right. Kitty's soft fluffy tail dangles down Jet's side. I watch it stiffen and jerk. Kitty is getting annoyed.

The smallest Taylor throws tantrums if he gets annoyed. We make great efforts to not annoy him because he throws plates and yowls. An annoyed Kitty could do much worse, much more, than that.

I back Lucky farther away. Poor Jinny, she's stuck on the same pony with him. No wonder she's so determined to stay calm!

Back in the tree house I figured a fun way to tell Jinny the plan. I was going to lead up slowly, tempt and tease, and finally reveal the plan like a trump card. But with Kitty's tail jerking almost under my nose, I lower my voice and say it flat out in one sentence.

Even so, Jinny is impressed. Deeply impressed. She murmurs, "Cosmic."

"Bingo," I say with satisfaction. I have never impressed Jinny before.

Softly, "That'll sure show them."

"Right."

Gently, "They'll never pester us again. They'll never come up the Hill again."

"You bet."

Jinny gathers her reins and turns Jet for home. Lucky and I amble abreast but at a distance. In motion again, Kitty relaxes. His eyes squeeze shut. He's like a toddler who sleeps best in a moving car.

Jinny says politely, "Hey, what was the idea this morning?"

"I thought I'd see if I could ride alone." And I could, too!

Sweet as honey, Jinny says, "You're lucky Kitty's here. Without Kitty here, they'd hear me yell downtown."

"Don't melt down. You were doing chores."

"When I saw that pony gone, I thought B and T stole her."

Of course. I should have known Jinny would think that.

Kitty must feel Jinny ready to explode. He opens his eyes and stiffens his tail.

"I'm sorry," I say sincerely. "I should have told you Lucky was with me."

"Yeah." Jinny nods.

"But don't orbit. Look at Kitty."

Jinny glances down at him and starts to sing.

"Rock-a-bye, Kitty

"On Jet's black back.

"When we get to the barn

"He'll have a fat snack."

And holy Honolulu! That quiets Kitty!

9

July 21
7 A.M.

"Turn over every leaf," Grandma says. "Don't miss a bean. Beans go tough when they're big."

We crawl down her endless garden row, facing each other across thick bush beans. Grandma has on old jeans with plastic tie-on kneepads, an old work shirt of Dad's, and a straw shade hat. I'm dressed for Lucky. Grandma caught me sneaking out the door and stuck this bean pail in my hand.

Now I sigh. "Why do we need more beans anyhow?"

It's good Grandma doesn't hear that. She's

59

been canning beans forever. Jars of beans crowd the cellar shelves. Before she's through, jars of carrots and corn and tomatoes will crowd the cellar floor, and my hands will be worn right through from picking.

My back aches already. I kneel up and stretch. Three young catbirds flutter in the hedge, learning to fly. A hawk circles over Rocky Rise, watching out for snakes. Hot sunlight deepens.

Grandma sits back on her heels. "You were in a hurry this morning, Alice. You're in a hurry most mornings." She watches my lips as I answer.

"I go riding."

"Well, I figured that."

I tell her proudly, "I can ride all alone now!"

"Without your friend?"

"Jinny has a lot of chores."

"Hmm. Maybe you need more chores yourself." I'm thankful to see Grandma's eyes twinkle under the shade hat. "And your friend doesn't mind if you ride off without her? She must be nicer than I thought."

"Jinny's nice."

"Just a bit bossy, eh?"

"Well, maybe a bit."

"And how are your other friends, B and T?"

A geyser of joy shoots up inside me. I bounce on my knees and shout, "We're going to laser them away!"

"What say?" Grandma was watching my lips. I shouted, but those words took her completely by surprise. Me, too.

Slower. "We've got a Great Evil Plan to teach them respect."

"My heavens!"

"It's my own plan, Grandma. It's a cosmic Great Evil Plan, and Kitty is in it."

"Kitty?" Grandma perks up like Lucky seeing a carrot.

"Kitty isn't a cat. He's a skunk."

"Promised land!"

"Jan O'Neal saved him when a car hit his mother. He's tame, but he's still got his stinker."

Slowly Grandma nods. Softly she repeats my dumb, thoughtless, stupid, betraying words. "Skunk. Stinker. Evil Plan." Her eyes turn sober under the shade hat. "Alice, I want to hear this plan."

"It's . . . it's a secret!" Too late now. Much too late.

When Grandma speaks like that it's no good to argue. She watches every word of the Evil

Plan as I shout it. If B and T are sneaking behind the hedge, they hear it, too. She listens and laughs, but at the end she shakes her head. "Alice, it's too mean."

"We've got to do something. You said yourself we should teach B and T respect."

"That's true. But this plan is like hiding a snake in a girl's desk. It's what you call overkill."

"They'll respect us forever."

"They'll hate you, too."

Joy, pride, and excitement whoosh out of me on a sigh.

Grandma says, "Let's think on it. Back to the beans."

She tips her shade hat to the sun and crawls along the row, humming "The Heavens Declare."

I pick slowly, sadly. I fall behind. Why did I ever open my stupid mouth?

Grandma breaks off humming. She kneels up and turns to me, beaming. "Alice! Listen to this. You said, remember, B and T were going to steal the horses. Well . . ."

Grandma's plan is still my cosmic Evil Plan, only scaled down. Softened.

"That will do it," she assures me. "And if

worse comes to worst, they can only blame themselves."

Slowly I nod.

"Alice, I don't want to hear later that any harm's been done."

Slowly I shake my head.

"This plan is not foolproof. Harm might come if you were careless."

"We won't be careless."

This plan will do. I'll make Jinny see that it will.

Grandma straightens her shade hat and bends to the beans. "Fill your pail halfway. Then you can go ride your—the new horse."

* * * * * * * * * * * * **10**

*J*inny and I lie side by side in the Mowing. We don't speak, we don't move. We almost don't breathe. A hawk circles high up, a cuckoo calls in the Orchard, mosquitoes whine. We lie here as if asleep.

We're used to this. We've been doing it for days, a short time each day.

Kitty is used to it, too. Kitty naps in a closed crate beside us, a feed sack thrown over it for shade.

Jet and Lucky are used to it, but they are not quiet like us. They're not supposed to be quiet. Tied to the oldest, biggest apple tree on the

Orchard edge, they whisk and shudder at flies, stamp and mutter. We can't see them through the tall grass that hides us, but we hear every mane-flap and tail-whisk.

Nearby, Deeper Voice says loudly, "Batman, there they are!"

Like fish to bait, like coons to garden corn, B and T have come. They're here. My stomach shudders. Jinny grabs both my hands in hers.

Whispers, rustles.

A pony stamps, a pony blows.

Twigs crack as B and T move in.

Deeper Voice says, "Maybe they bite."

Squeaker says, "You grab him under the chin so he can't bite."

Deeper Voice, "This one looks tamer. He's mine."

Jinny squeezes my hands. A light goes on in her face. Her freckles shine.

Squeaker, "Hey, look, they're all bridled for us! I'm riding mine."

I want to leap up and yell, Get your paws off my Lucky! But Jinny leans on my hands.

Deeper Voice, "Go ahead, ride. I'll lead this one . . . if I can."

They've got the ponies untied. They're all set to go.

Jinny rises up out of the grass. "Hold it," she shouts. "That's enough of that!"

I shove the feed sack off Kitty's crate. Hot sunlight wakes Kitty and annoys him. I stand up behind Jinny.

Bones holds Jet's bridle. Tubs hops beside Lucky, all set to scramble aboard. I go hot with rage.

Tall Bones is so neat you might think he was nice. Jeans clean, brown hair combed, he grins at us across the high grass.

Short Tubs's pants are ripped. Twigs stick in his black curls. He pops a huge gum bubble at us.

Bones says cheerily, "Our turn to ride, kids. What'cha going to do about it?" Bones is Deeper Voice.

That's it. They've brought it on themselves, it's all their own fault. If they had not tried to steal the ponies this would not happen now.

Jinny stoops. She scoops Kitty up in her arms and straightens up.

Now is the time for care and caution and making no mistake.

Dad says that a skunk can blind you if he shoots off his stinker close to your eyes. It doesn't last. You get your sight back after a while. But we don't want it happening to us, or even, actually, to B and T. That would be overkill.

My original Great Evil Plan was this. We would hunt down B and T, ride up to them, dump Kitty on their heads and gallop off. But Grandma reminded me of this blinding business. She thought it was too mean, and I guess it was. This plan is working nicely. And it will be all their own fault!

B and T turn pale. Tubs pops his gum bubble back inside his mouth. Bones steps away, dragging Jet with him. Jet plants his hoofs and objects. Bones lets go.

Jinny marches slowly toward them. I follow, watching Kitty's tail stiffen and jerk. Kitty is decidedly annoyed. He doesn't like the hot sun, these strange humans, or the meltdown he feels from Jinny.

Jinny says to Tubs, "Let that pony go."

Now we stand with Bones and Tubs in the apple tree shade. According to Grandma's plan, if they turn the ponies loose we have to let B and T go. I hope they don't! I hope they argue! I hope—

Bones croaks, "Batman and Robin, Chief!" He seems to be talking to Jinny.

Tubs squeaks, "No fair!"

Calmly Jinny says, "No fair stealing pets. Let that pony go."

Tubs's answer is, he grabs Lucky's mane and starts to climb her side.

I yell.

Bones cries, "Tom! Don't—"

Jinny steps forward and dumps Kitty, not too gently, between B and T.

Kitty goes into his dance. He stomps one front foot and then the other and turns to face us, away from B and T. His tail rises stiff in the air.

Bones turns and runs.

Wild-eyed, Tubs scrabbles at Lucky's side. She rears and plunges.

We turn and run down the middle track through the Mowing.

Hoofs pound as Jet and Lucky rush away.

Behind us, for the first time in his sheltered life, Kitty shoots off his famous stinker.

Blast off! If that is all the skill he needs to live as a wild animal, Kitty will do just fine.

July 28
11 A.M.

*J*inny, listen."

We are picking blueberries for the O'Neals to sell in Granton. Jinny picks fast, two-handed. She rolls berries into the coffee can slung around her neck without hardly looking at them. I hold back branches with one hand and pick with the other. Berries still *ping!* as they drop into my coffee can because it's mostly empty. But that's because Jinny just emptied both our cans into the pail at the end of the row.

Voices sound nearby. People pick their own berries at O'Neals' lot. We hear the voices of old folks, kids, and a baby. But we don't see anyone through the thick, high bushes.

Earlier Lucky and Jet grazed side by side down the center aisle. Now they stand in the shade of a line maple and flick flies off each other's faces with their tails.

"Jinny, look. I mean this."

Jinny won't like it. I can still back down and not say it.

Jinny says, "Huh?" and eats a fat berry.

I just know Jinny is going to melt down. But still I have to say this. The time to say it has come.

"I want to get paid for the berries I pick."

"What?" Jinny widens her eyes at me around the bush as her two hands dive in, picking.

I point out, "You get paid."

"I pick gallons more berries than you do!"

"Okay. So you should get paid more. But I want my share. It's like when we baby-sit. I mop up the milk, and you get paid. Not fair."

"I thought you liked to baby-sit with me!"

"I do."

"Well, then."

"But from now on I want my fair share. You

know, come winter I'll have to buy Lucky's hay."

"Honolulu!" Jinny says crossly. Her face stiffens. "I won't get many jobs if people have to pay extra."

For several breaths we pick silently. Then I say, "Maybe we should work separate jobs."

Jinny stops picking. Her freckles stand out like gold coins. Like Kitty, Jinny is getting annoyed. If she had a black-and-white tail it would rise, right now. "Work separate jobs! Alice Brown, what do you think you can do without me?"

That's exactly what I need to find out.

"What would you do all by yourself if a baby swallowed a pin?"

"I don't know right now, but—"

"Bet your life you don't know! What would you do if a pot caught fire?"

"Look, Jinny—"

"Who do you think you are, Alice Brown?"

Now Jinny shoots into orbit.

She stands clear of the bush and glares at me like I'm a snake in the bush.

I stand clear. I go into orbit. I cry, "Yes!"

Nearby voices have fallen silent. People up

and down the blueberry rows are listening to us fight.

"Yes!" Jinny shouts. "What's that mean, 'Yes'?"

"It means, yes, I think I'm Alice Brown!"

"You'll find out! I'm the one with the brains around here! You won't get far without me!"

"Oh yeah? Who thought up the Great Evil Plan, you, Jinny O'Neal?"

"Yes, me! I think up everything! I do everything! You'll find that out!"

Panting with rage, we stare at each other. The hot blueberry lot holds its breath, listening.

More softly, Jinny growls, "Don't call me and I won't call you."

"Bingo!" I rip the coffee can off my neck and hurl it under the bush. Berries spill around the roots.

Jinny snarls. "And get your fleabag miracle pony off O'Neal land. See what you can do with her by yourself."

I turn on my heel as they say in books and stride down the center aisle to Lucky.

From the corner of my eye I see pickers in blueberry aisles. They all stare at me. There's an old couple stiffly picking high-bush. There's a fat woman with a baby crawling beside her, another with two toddlers sucking thumbs. All of them, even the crawling baby, stare at me like I'm on a soap opera. They all heard every word Jinny and I yelled.

Before Lucky sees me coming I grab her bridle and scramble aboard. Too late she plants her hoofs and blows. I'm giving the orders. Heads high, we trot up the center aisle. The pickers stare again, but this time they smile. All that good O'Neal grass and grooming have turned Lucky pretty. Her coat shines. Her mane floats. Jinny said she would turn out pretty. As usual, Jinny was right.

But what am I going to do with Lucky now that Jinny's thrown her out?

Clear of the blueberry lot, we canter through the Mowing into Old Pasture. The rainbow of bright, small flowers has faded here. Thickets of tall, straight ironweeds bud, goldenrod and Joe Pye—Dad's favorite flowers. We canter through the thickets and up Rocky Rise.

Lucky arcs her neck and blows happily. She knows it's a bright day and we're cantering. She doesn't know that she and Jet are through. She'll never graze with him again or pester him or whisk flies off his face. But she doesn't guess that.

Sweat runs down my face as I draw rein on top of Rocky Rise. I can't see my house through this flowing sweat, or Granton down below.

I won't ride with Jinny again. I won't follow her through Orchard or Sugar Bush or down to Taylors'. What's she in orbit for? Did I ask too much?

Honolulu, I just wanted my fair share!

This isn't sweat I can't see through. This is tears.

I leave the reins loose. Lucky turns her way and walks along the ridge and where she wants. I can't see where because I'm crying like Niagara Falls.

At least I don't have to look out for B and T! My idea cooked their goose well-done. No matter that Jinny thinks it was her idea. She would!

Jinny would never dream of working without pay. Why should I? Why did I?

Because Jinny is such fun when she's nice. Because I liked Jinny a lot. Still do, actually.

I ought to blink these tears away and gallop

all the way to Blueberry Lot, say I didn't mean it.

Only I did mean it. Still do, actually.

My rainbow stands inside my head, bright and broad. Because of my rainbow I can't take back what I said. What I said was true.

Lucky stops, blows, and drops her head.

I wipe my eyes on my T-shirt and see, as though under water, a stone wall, a line maple, and my tree house.

Lucky knew where to come.

I slide down, take off her bridle, and hang it on a branch. "Thanks, Lucky. You go graze. I'll be upstairs." I climb the rope ladder and collapse on my tree house floor.

I think and cry and think.

I've lost Jinny.

I still have Lucky. What am I going to do with her?

I'll have to find jobs somehow, somewhere, to feed her. And what will I do if a baby swallows a pin?

Whatever happens I have to keep Lucky. Lucky's my friend. She's the most luck I've ever had, and she depends on me.

And what about Dad's NO ANIMALS rule?

My eyes ache from crying.

What's that noise?

It's been going on for a while, and I just didn't listen. Now I listen. It's soft and steady, like the hiss of an electric clock. It's crickets.

I sit up and look out the door.

The first crickets are starting to sing. Crickets mean fall is coming, and winter comes after fall, and what am I going to do about Lucky?

Jinny and I had Lucky's winter planned. She would stay in O'Neals' barn with Cow and Speckles Calf and Jet, safe from wind and snow. I would pay O'Neals for her hay, somehow. I still have to do that, but now I don't have a barn.

I won't cry any more. My eyes are just starting to see. And what they see is something moving way out in Old Pasture.

Jinny's looking for me! She wants to make up! She—

That's a human being out there, but it's on foot.

It's coming pretty straight this way through the budding goldenrod.

It can't mean to come here! Nobody knows

about this tree house but me—and whoever left fresh, sticky gum here.

Honolulu! It's the gum sticker!

It's a He. I know that by his straightforward, arm-swinging stride.

He's got brown hair. He's thin and neat in jeans and T-shirt.

He's Bones.

* * * * * * * * * * * * **12**

July 28
1 P.M.

Where is Bones going with his straightforward stride?

Right here. Straight toward this maple he swings, looking right at me through the leaves. He can't see me yet, but he's definitely aiming for this tree house.

I am unarmed. I have no Kitty here to dance and threaten, no Jinny to stand out front, not even a stick to brandish.

I could maybe climb down, run for Lucky, and gallop out of here. There's still a few minutes for that. But I'm not sure exactly where Lucky is. And if she doesn't want to be caught

. . . Honolulu, how embarrassing! Me chasing Lucky, and Bones chasing me!

While I think desperately, Bones swings closer.

I grab the rope ladder, haul it up, and coil it stiffly on the tree house floor. That's all the defense I can think of.

Bones comes steadily on. Almost inside the maple shade he stops midstride. Hc has seen Lucky off grazing by herself and her bridle dangling near his nose.

Bones reaches up and taps the bridle so it swings. He moves on into the shade and looks up at me in the tree house door. Our eyes meet.

Bones's eyes do not glare. They meet mine quietly. His deep voice does not growl or even crack. Calmly he asks me, "Where's Chief?"

My voice quavers as I ask him, "Where's Tubs?"

"Tom's home with spots."

"Who's Spots?"

"Spots and fever. Have you got Stinker up there?"

I hiccup a silly, nervous giggle. "Kitty went wild."

"So he was tame! I thought so."

"Yes, he was Jan O'Neal's pet. But since . . . since then, he's . . . gone wild."

"Good. You got Chief hiding up there?"

"You mean Jinny? No." Blast off, he would know if Jinny were here!

Bones smiles a slow, thoughtful smile. "You up there by yourself?"

"Um . . ."

I've got the rope ladder up here. Bones can most likely climb the tree if he really wants to, but I could push him off.

He's got Lucky down there. He could take the bridle and go catch her, but I know he doesn't know horses. We're sort of even.

I don't like admitting I'm here alone, but Bones has guessed that.

I nod.

"Look, Alice Brown, you're by yourself. I'm by myself. We can have a truce."

"How the— How do you know my name?"

"I know a lot about you."

"From spying!"

Bones is not embarrassed. He nods. "Can I come up?"

I think, Not by the hair of my chinny chin chin, and hiccup another giggle.

Bones says, "Look. No crossed fingers." He holds his hands out so I can see. "Let's have a truce. You hungry?"

"Huh?" This takes me sort of by surprise. Yes, I am hungry! I left my lunch at Blueberry Lot. Chalk one up for Jinny.

"I got a sandwich or two here."

"What do you want to come up for?"

"Cooler there." That's so. There's always a breeze in the maple leaves. "Besides, that's my tree house. You're trespassing."

"I am not! It is not! This is my tree house. My secret. Nobody knows about it but me."

"It's been my secret for months. Well, neither of us really owns it, you know. So let's share it."

"Share it?" There's not much room up here. Even skinny Jinny would be a tight squeeze.

"I've got lunch and a Space Spider. Come on, Al, let down the rope."

My hand reaches for the rope.

This is crazy.

I look down into Bones's eyes, which seem simple and honest, like Jet's eyes.

Who was it in the story who let down the rope of her hair? Rapunzel. Rapunzel didn't really know the prince, but she took a chance. She threw her long, long hair out the window for him to climb.

Feeling a bit like Rapunzel, I uncoil the rope out the door. It drops and dangles.

Bones takes hold and climbs.

* * * * * * * * * * * * **13**

July 28

2 P.M.

I draw back into the tree house and fold up my legs. Bones settles in by the door. We study each other suspiciously.

Bones says, "You got spots. You feel okay?"

My eyes must be all red and puffy. Quickly I say, "Fine!"

"Sure." But Bones knows I've been crying. "Have a sandwich."

From his jeans pockets he pulls three plastic-wrapped messes. "Peanut butter. Apple butter. Cream cheese. You pick."

My stomach says, Hungry! My eyes say, Ick!

These sandwiches have been sat on, rolled on, and thumped.

"Um . . . Guess not. Thanks."

"Good." From his T-shirt pocket Bones pulls a small comic book. "You like Space Spider, Al?"

"Nobody ever called me that before!"

"What, Space Spider?"

"Al."

"Okay if I do?"

"Sure." Actually, I like it.

"You, Al. Me, Harry."

"Harry."

"That's a good way to start a truce. With names."

Bones—Harry—rips Space Spider in half and hands me the front half. "I've read that." He opens the back half, drops his nose into it, and pretends to read. Reading, he gobbles all three sandwiches the way Lucky gobbles carrots.

I pretend to read. But it's weird, being squashed in here with Bones—Harry.

He smells Boy, like Lucky smells Horse. We have a truce. I'm not scared of him, at least not right now. So I can see he's not that bad-looking.

I've just lost one friend. Can I maybe, just maybe, make another friend?

Harry says suddenly, "Al, that Stinker thing was mean."

Right away I stick up for myself. I'm going to stick up for myself from now on so people don't get me wrong, like Jinny did. I say, "Remember how you tripped Jet up with a rope?"

"Nobody got hurt."

"Remember how you stole our lunch?"

"You oughtn't leave your lunch on a rock! If we didn't steal it, a coon would."

"How about that Evil Plan to steal our ponies?"

"Ha ha! So you were there in the grass, like I thought! That was mostly a joke." So Dad was right about that. "But that Stinker thing . . . We had to throw our clothes away, Al."

"Ha ha!"

"Not funny, Al. We had to wash in tomato juice."

"Like you said, no one got hurt."

Bones—Harry—gives me a serious look over the top of Space Spider. "Want to make peace? A truce is good, but peace is better."

"Sure. Absolutely." I speak from the heart.

"Tom won't mind. But there's still Chief."

"No, there isn't. There's just me."

"Batman! What happened?"

"Oh, Jinny's okay. She didn't break her neck or anything like that."

Maybe Harry mumbles, "Too Bad." I almost don't hear.

I lean back into the spider-webbed wall. I tell Harry what happened. In the telling it seems much shorter and simpler than in the happening.

Harry laughs. "Chief's forgotten the whole thing by now."

"Uh-uh." I shake my head. "Right now she's collecting the money for the berries I picked. So tell me what you think, Harry. What can I do with Lucky now?"

I don't really expect Harry to give the problem a thought. Why should he?

But he frowns, feels in his T-shirt, and pulls out a packet of gum. Silently he holds it out to me. I push it gently away.

Harry takes a stick of gum and chews. Chewing, he thinks. After thinking, he says, "There's an old shed right behind your house."

"Filthy." Dirtier than this tree house!

"Clean it."

"Door won't shut."

"I know that." Huh? "There's a board gone in the door, too. Doesn't matter. Fix a bar."

"Lucky's my secret. My folks can't see her."

"Secret?" Now, that surprises Harry! "How come secret?"

"My dad's got this NO ANIMALS rule. We can't even have a cat at our house, never mind a pony!"

"Batman! How come?"

"Animals cost. They eat and see the vet."

Harry frowns, chews, pops gum. Then he says, "Look, Al. There's a hedge between the shed and your house. That'll hide your horse pretty well—for a while. If anyone sees her you can say you're keeping her for Chief."

That's a thought.

"Tell you what," says Harry. "You clean up the shed. I'll fix the bar."

I don't believe my ears. "You'll what? Why?"

"I'll make it so the door shuts on the horse. I've got nothing much doing, with Tom home with spots."

I stare at Harry.

He laughs at me through a huge gum bubble. "It's no big deal."

"Seems . . . pretty big . . . to me." Seems cosmic. What sort of friend am I finding here?

"Won't take a half hour. You have someplace to put Lucky tonight?"

I've got that figured out. "She can stay in O'Neals' Back Field with Jet. I'll take her in late, get her out early. Jinny won't see her. She'll stay right with Jet."

"You're sure right about that!"

"Huh?"

"Me and Tom used to watch those horses." Harry means they used to spy on them. "They were never farther than they could whisk each other. Okay. So I'll meet you at your shed, oh, ten o'clock tomorrow. Your dad'll be working. Your grandma won't hear us."

What doesn't Harry know?

The sun is low, and I'm starved when I go to catch Lucky.

"Looky, Lucky! Looky, Lucky!"

She lifts her head, smells no carrot. So she goes back to grazing. Only each time I get near she trots away.

Harry calls, "Ten o'clock!" and goes off with his straightforward stride. He doesn't wait around to see me look silly.

Grandma must be watching out the door for me. Dad will be home any minute. I can't chase Lucky around Old Pasture all night.

I stop. "Looky, Lucky, you win. Stay here tonight." Nothing will happen to her. "I'll bring a carrot tomorrow."

I walk away.

Bingo. Hoofbeats behind me. Lucky mutters, tosses her mane, and breathes down my neck.

I bridle her, mount, and turn toward Back Field.

* * * * * * * * * * * * **14**

July 29
7 A.M.

*L*ast night I took Lucky's bridle off just about here and hung it on this birch.

Bingo. Here it is. I take it down and creep carefully through the crumbled stone wall into Back Field.

Early mists drift and curl. There's no sign of Jinny. Out in the middle, Lucky pesters Jet.

He wants to graze before it gets hot. She wants to play. She circles Jet with her mischievous, teasing trot. She flicks her tail in his face, nudges his shoulder, and nickers softly.

Jet reminds me of a patient baby-sitter. Bigger and slower than Lucky, he watches her kindly. Once in a while she pesters too much and he nips her. Like now.

Lucky wheels and gallops half the field away.

Relieved, Jet drops nose to grass.

Lucky circles back. Small hoofs drumming, tail flying, she charges past his nose. I bet that doesn't help the flavor of the grass.

Jet whinnies crossly and gives chase. Just what Lucky wants. They thunder toward me. Galloping, Jet forgets he's cross. Galloping takes him over. Legs stretch, neck arches. He shrills happily.

I watch, bridle in one hand, carrot in the other. Something inside me stretches and arches, too. The rainbow inside me brightens.

Lucky is my miracle. Any work or problem she costs me will be worth it. I'll clean that filthy shed for her. I'll do whatever it takes to keep Lucky.

She sees me and veers away. She gallops back toward the far gate, Jet close on her heels.

I walk out into the mist. "Looky, Lucky!"

Near the gate both ponies stop, turn, and watch me. Ears prick. Manes shake. Each pony is thinking about this one carrot in my hand.

I snap it in half. "Looky, Lucky!"

A misty figure drifts into the field. Tall and

skinny, it holds carrot and bridle out from its sides. It stops and looks from the ponies to me.

Floating mist softens Jinny's outline. A ray of sunshine touches her wild red hair. I can't see if she smiles. Maybe she does. Maybe—

I call, "Hey, Jinny!" and wave my bridle.

Jinny lets loose with a screeching whistle.

Jet trots right up behind her and crunches his carrot. Jinny grabs his halter.

With a thunder of hoofs, Lucky is gone.

Now what? I can't melt into the mist. But just maybe I can still make peace, or at least a truce.

Jinny comes slowly toward me, hauling Jet. One step and another and another. When we stand nose to nose Jinny snaps, "Well, Alice Brown?"

We stand on her family's land. She owns the bridle I hold.

She says, "Guess you didn't mean all that low-level trash, huh?"

But I did mean every word I said. I still mean it. The rainbow shines steadily inside me. I look into Jinny's angry eyes and say, "I meant it, Jinny O'Neal."

For an instant she looks disappointed. Then her sharp chin comes up. "You're really going to fight me about money?" The way she says it, you'd think money meant nothing to Jinny.

"Not just money," I tried to explain. "Fairness."

"After all the stuff I've done for you!"

"What about the stuff I've done for you?"

"Huh! Like what?"

"Like all that baby-sitting! All those berries!"

Actually, I did more than that for Jinny. I loved Jinny. I followed her like Lucky follows Jet. When she laughed at my T-shirt I wrecked it. When she liked her hairstyle on me, I wore it. But there's no way in the world to say all that, and the new Me wouldn't say it anyhow.

Jinny shrugs. "You sure like the taste of money, Alice Brown."

"You like money yourself."

"Not that much."

"Fine. Then pay me what I earned yesterday."

Jinny speaks slowly, softly, like she's talking to a small Taylor. "Some things are more important than money. Things like, um, friendship."

I couldn't agree more! I would dearly love to be Jinny's friend again forever. But the new Me says coldly, "Bingo, Jinny O'Neal."

Jinny turns her back. She bridles Jet, climbs

up, and gathers her reins. From up there she looks down on me.

"Okay, Alice Brown, we're through. Get your lousy, flea-bit pony off my land. And watch out with that bridle. My grandpa had that bridle. It's rotten, like you."

With a quick, mean jerk she turns Jet. His tail flicks and stings my face as he trots away.

July 29
11 A.M.

*I*f I had time," Harry says through a gum bubble, "and if I had a board I'd stick it in here." He points to the gap between the shed door and the jamb. "But it won't matter. Your horse can't squeeze through there."

He squats outside the door, choosing tools out of a battered lunchbox. "See this here hasp?" He holds up a lean scrap of wood. "This'll fall into this here latch, which I'll put here." On the jamb. "That'll hold her." Chewing, he drills holes in door and jamb.

"Tell you something, Al. You're going to

have to buy that horse hay, if you can't leave her loose. I asked Tom about that."

Bingo, Harry. I kneel in the grass and look into the lunch box, where weird blades gleam. Jinny probably knows all their names.

Lucky grazes, tied to the hedge with a long rope Harry brought. He also brought her a water pail, with strict instructions from Tubs—Tom. "Don't ever leave the handle up, Al. She can catch her head under it and drown." But Jinny told me that, long ago.

Grandma went off to a Seniors' lunch down in Granton. Friends came up and drove off with her. That makes things extra easy for now. Even Grandma might have heard Harry's hammer if she'd been here.

"So," Harry asks me, "how're you going to buy hay?"

"Have to find some jobs."

"I got a cousin wants a baby-sitter. Let's see the screwdriver, Al."

I lean to the tools. Screwdriver. That's one I know. I find it and hand it over.

I say, "Maybe Lucky can graze on your rope for a while." Tied out all over the place.

"They'd see her for sure. And you don't want

to leave her tied out by herself. She can wind herself up and choke."

More wisdom from Tubs. Tom.

"Too bad you had to go fight with Chief. You had a real nice deal there."

"Sure. Except I worked a lot for free."

"You got something for free, too. Ever think of that? You could work out a deal. Chief does something. You do something. It's called barter."

He's right.

"Make it up, Al."

I shake my head. "I tried." Sort of.

"Okay, you're going to have to hustle. I got a brother-in-law who— No, that's going to be my job. Let's see the left-handed wrench."

"You aren't left-handed." That I know.

"Let's see it."

Shapes and points gleam up at me. Left-handed wrench. If I could find the right-handed wrench I might know what I was looking for.

Harry laughs. "Al, there's no such thing as a left-handed wrench!"

I give him a sour look.

"Here, hold this for me."

I stand up with Harry and hold the bar—hasp—against the door while he screws it in.

"There," he says proudly. "That'll hold her

but good." He lifts the bar and drops it into the latch. Lifts and drops. "See that?"

Humbly, gratefully, I say, "It's great."

"It'll do the job."

"Bingo." Lucky will look out through that gap and see rain and snow and ice, and feel safe inside her shed.

"You got a Coke, Al?"

"Oh, sure! Come on in."

Harry takes out his gum and pounds it onto the shed door like a signature. I'll handle that later.

Right now I lead Harry through the hedge gap, up the porch steps, and into the kitchen. The place is cool and quiet, neat like Grandma. I rustle up Cokes, bread, baloney, mayo.

Then I notice Harry staring around like he's just been dropped on Mars.

He opens the Coke I hand him and points around the room. "Where'd all that stuff come from?"

He means Grandma's curtains embroidered with cats and the rose garden tablecloth.

"My grandma embroiders for fun. It's her hobby."

"She made all that?"

"She embroidered it."

"Well, my rotted socks! She got more stuff?"

"Just every curtain and bedspread and bureau scarf in the house."

I open my own Coke. "Sit down, Harry. Fix a sandwich."

We sit down and dive in. Between gulps Harry says, "I got an aunt starting a new store downtown. Going to sell crafts. Stuff like that." He nods at the embroidered cats. "For millions."

"Millions?"

"Well, for a lot. Your grandma sell this stuff?"

"Never has." The rose garden tablecloth seems to glow with a whole new light.

"Maybe she could meet my aunt."

"Great idea. Then Grandma could keep a cat."

Harry shrugs. "Sure, if that's what she wants. Bet she could do a lot of things."

"I could get her Jan O'Neal's tricolored kitten. I mean, if I was speaking to Jinny. Want another Coke?"

"I'll take one."

"Me, too." I get up and open the fridge.

Behind me Harry says, "Me and Tom used to call you Me, Too."

Did I hear that right? I pick out two Cokes, nudge the fridge shut, and turn to Harry. "What?"

"Me, Too was your name. Your pal was Chief. You were Me, Too."

Gently I set the Cokes down on the rose garden. "Me, Too?"

"Well, you did everything she did. She went first. You came after. She talked. You listened. I didn't know you were anybody, Al, till yesterday."

In the air between Harry and me I see a sort of dream-movie of Jinny and me, the way B and T saw us. Across a field of Indian paints and daisies I see Jinny bounce to Jet's gallop, red hair flying. Just behind her, I bounce on Lucky, brown hair flying. Jinny and Jet veer downhill out of sight. Lucky and I follow.

Chief and Me, Too.

Well, my rotted socks!

* * * * * * * * * * * * **16**

July 30
5 P.M.

*T*here," says Grandma, panting a little. "That's the most of it. Now you can look."

She plunks the small bathroom mirror down on the table before me.

Rain drums on the window. Irish stew simmers on the stove. My thick, brown hair lies around my chair like a shorn sheep's fleece.

I'm scared to look. I look at the scissors on the table, then at the magazine with the short-haired girl and the Honda. I look up into Grandma's anxious face. Anywhere but in the mirror.

Grandma rubs her aching wrists and nods urgently at the mirror.

Finally, I pick it up and look.

This is not me.

This person is trim. Her brown hair swings shoulder length, fringed across the forehead. Her brown eyes are steady and cool. She holds her chin up. She's not the Alice Brown I've always been.

This is the girl who wouldn't cave in and tell Jinny she didn't really mean all that low-level trash after all. This girl made peace with Bones and will take care of Lucky. This girl is Al.

"My heavens!" Grandma bursts out. "Don't you like it at all?"

"Oh yes. Yes, I do."

"I think it's you."

"So do I."

"I think you look nicer than the girl in the ad."

"Thanks, Grandma. Are you through?"

"Promised land, no! Now for the trim-up. Hold still."

I hold the mirror and watch. Grandma snips here and there, humming "Go Forth to Life" and frowning.

"Grandma?"

"What say?" The scissors pause.

"There's a new craft store going to open in Granton."

"What?" Grandma watches my lips in the mirror.

Louder. "A new store in Granton. Someone told me you could sell your embroidery there for millions."

"Millions?"

"For enough to keep a cat. This here's too long, Grandma."

I point. Grandma snips. In the mirror I see her face soften as she thinks about a cat.

I think about Lucky, safe and dry in her shed. I bet she's watching this hard rain through the gap in the door.

I think about Jinny, my lost friend. I'm mad at Jinny. I'm in orbit, melted down. Jinny wasn't fair.

But I know, deep inside, I will always miss her.

Riding alone is great, just Lucky and me and the sky. But sometimes I start to say, "Hey, Jinny!" and there's no answer.

And Lucky misses Jet. Every so often she lets out a neigh to wake the Hill. Then her ears twitch for Jet's answer. And there's no answer.

"There." Grandma puts the scissors down. She combs my new, surprisingly light hairstyle and fluffs it with her hand. "Look," she says. "The rain's stopped. Let's go see if there's a rainbow."

She trips to the back door and out on the porch.

I can't get used to Al. I'm studying Al in the mirror when Grandma calls, "Alice, come quick! Before it fades."

I jump and run.

The rainbow rises by O'Neals'. It arches across Rocky Rise and vanishes in midair. It shimmers and glimmers like Grandma's eyes watching it.

Lucky pushes through the hedge gap to our side.

Harry said she couldn't squeeze through the door. But I should have known that my smart Lucky could poke her nose through and jiggle the hasp. No great trick for her.

Here she comes out on the lawn and looks up at us. Seeing no carrot, she shakes her mane, blows, and drops her nose to the wet grass.

"Ooooh!" I shout in Grandma's ear. "*Look* at the rainbow! Just *look* at it!"

Grandma says, "Alice. There's a horse in the yard."

"Ah? Um?"

"It's the accident pony, isn't it. Your pony."

Back in the house the front screen door bangs. Tired footsteps trudge down the hall to the kitchen. Grandma doesn't hear the footsteps. If I were the old Alice Brown I might burst into tears right now.

The new Al says calmly, "Yes. She's mine."

Dad comes out on the porch with us. He calls, "Mom!"

Grandma shies.

"Sorry," he says. "I hoped you were seeing the rainbow."

He turns to me. His face goes all stiff. Warning lights glow in his eyes. "Alice," he rumbles like distant thunder. "What's that animal doing in our yard?"

* * * * * * * * * * * * **17**

July 30
6 P.M.

Grandma sneaks a thin arm around my shoulders. Bravely she says, "Just look at her, Dave! Pretty as the rainbow."

Dad snorts.

Lucky looks up and around. That snort sounded like Jet to her. Seeing no Jet, she goes back to grazing.

Dad glares at me.

Grandma squeezes my shoulders so I can hardly breathe. She says, "Dave, you remember the accident at Taylors' where a truck turned over? Your brave daughter here rescued that horse off the truck."

Dad snarls. "You went messing about in that accident? You idiot, you were that crazy?"

Grandma says, "She saw the horse needed help."

"Mom," Dad growls. "Let the girl speak for herself." He scowls at me. "Lot of glass in the road. I heard about it. You had no business in the world messing about there."

Grandma says, "Love, Dave. She did it for love."

"She never saw the animal before in her life!"

"Love at first sight."

All this time I can't speak because Grandma's squeezing me so hard. I bet her arm will hurt later.

"What did you do," Dad asks me, "steal it while everyone was helping the driver?"

Now I have to speak. I wriggle Grandma's arm loose and cry, "No, Dad, of course not! He gave her to me."

"What!"

"He said—" I gasp. Grandma lets go of me. "He said he was taking her for dog meat . . . and now he had no place to put her."

Both Grandma and Dad look briefly shocked. They both glance out at Lucky who grazes happily, showing them her prettiest, cutest self. You wouldn't think those golden, heavy-lashed eyes could glitter with mischief.

Dad whistles. "Gave it to you. Must be totally, absolutely worthless. Is it lame, or what?"

"She's just fine." Old Alice Brown would be drowning in tears by now. Al speaks calmly.

Grandma says, "Look at her. Worth a million."

Lucky raises her head and poses. Her white mane and tail float like milkweed fluff. Her smooth coat glows red against the wet, green hedge. Behind her, the rainbow fades.

Dad mutters, "Who fed it up to look like that?"

Grandma tells him quickly, "Cheapest pet in the world, a pony in summer."

"And what about winter? I'm not buying hay!"

I say, "I'll take care of it."

Dad turns angry eyes back to me. "How?"

"I'll get jobs. I'm looking into it now."

Dad looks and looks at me. The anger in his eyes turns to surprise. "You've changed."

"We cut my hair. Just now."

"More than that." Dad studies me. Alice

Brown would look away or down at the floor. Not Al.

Dad sighs. "Al," he says, "sit down."

Dad recognizes Al!

I sink into the nearest plastic chair. Dad sits in the hammock loosely, big hands spread on knees. Grandma folds her arms and leans against the porch railing. She watches both our lips.

Dad says, "Let's hear the whole story."

I tell the whole story, every chapter and verse of it. I finish off with, "I call her Lucky because she's the most luck I've ever had. I brought her luck, and she brought me luck."

Dad says, "More than luck. She brought you more than luck, Al. She's changed you." He turns to Grandma. "Mom, I have a feeling you knew some of this, before."

Grandma smiles. "What say?"

Dad smiles his very rare smile. It starts off slow, like a rainy morning. Then it brightens like sun coming through.

I'm breathing funny, fast and shallow. My shoulders hurt from Grandma's grip. But watching Dad smile, I begin to feel that luck is still with Lucky and me. It's like a second miracle.

Dad says to me, "I didn't know how much you wanted it. You know, I'm always either down at the shop or thinking about the shop. I don't know what goes on here."

I nod. I understand that.

"Actually, I'm getting a raise. You can even miss a hay payment if times get rough."

Did I hear that right? Yes, I did. I swallow hard. "Dad, are you saying Lucky can stay?"

"Yes, I'm saying that. You want a contract?"

I nod.

Dad leans forward and takes my hand in his big, rough hand. "Lucky can stay as long as you do your best to take care of her in every way. You get sick days, cost of living. That's the best contract you'll ever see, Al."

Gravely we shake.

Grandma pipes up. "Does Lucky bite?"

"Sometimes, Grandma. If she's playing, she nips."

"Then you handle her, Alice. She's heading for my beans."

August 15
9 A.M.

*L*ucky pushes through thickets of goldenrod, Joe Pye, and purple milkweed. All these are Dad's favorite flowers—tall and tough—the same that bloom now, finally, about our gate. They bloom out here in Old Pasture, too, with no weeding or watering. That's why Dad likes them. They take care of themselves.

Petals and fluff spangle my jeans and Lucky's coat. We'll both need a good brush-up later. Crickets sing and hop from under Lucky's hoofs. Far and high, a hawk screams.

Away by Rocky Rise a happy whinny

shakes the air. Lucky stops dead and perks her ears.

"Yes," I tell her. "That's old Jet. He must have smelled you." For the wind drifts from us, that way.

Jet whinnies again, closer. Lucky tosses her mane, answers, and takes off without a sign from me. I bounce on her back like a sack of laundry as she takes her own way through the goldenrod.

Another whinny, another answer. Lucky breaks from walk to trot. Over purple milkweed I see Jinny's red hair flop, then Jet's black mane.

Jinny's face is pale and tight. She does not smile. Neither do I.

Jet trumpets, Lucky shrills. Both ponies rise to a canter. Clods and stones fly under hoofs. We tear through the milkweed. We canter together and stop. Lucky and Jet push foreheads together and squeal for joy.

I could almost do the same, I'm so thrilled to see Jinny. It's like I lost half of myself, and now I've got it back. Or have I?

Jinny says, so softly I can hardly hear her over the ponies' squeals, "Hey, Alice."

I answer softly. "Hey, Jinny."

"I got your berry money."

Berry money? Oh, yes. Berry money.

Jinny pulls a crushed, smeared envelope out of her jeans. I take it and stuff it into mine. "Thanks." I don't look at it.

"You cut your hair."

"Cooler this way."

"I bet." Jinny looks at me sort of like Dad did, that evening on the porch. She seems to see Al, too, just the way he did.

The ponies rear and buck. We pull them back apart. Jinny says, "They're glad to meet."

"So am I." I admit it.

Now Jinny smiles. "Me, too. Hey, what are you laughing at?"

"Nothing. I'm not laughing. I'm just happy." Maybe someday, far off, I might tell Jinny about Chief and Me, Too. But I doubt it.

"Jet would like it," Jinny says, "if Lucky came back in Back Field with him."

"Mmmm. She's got her own home." That home cost Harry and me some work.

"I bet she'd love to be with Jet."

Bingo. She sure would. And it would be a lot easier on me, not to pull grass all day to feed her. Not to mention cleaning out! But I don't want to sound too eager. "Mmmm. Maybe we could work out a barter deal. I help you baby-sit for hay, something like that."

"Bingo," says Jinny. "Come on, let's race."

"Yaaah, Lucky!"

"Yaaah, Jet!"

I loosen reins and lean forward. Lucky dashes ahead of Jet. She's younger, lighter, maybe even happier. Wind lifts our mane and hair. Clods fly. Goldenrod bends. Lucky and I fly up Rocky Rise to the sky.

About the Author

ANNE ELIOT CROMPTON has raised ponies and goats, and painted wildlife. Born to Ethel Cook Eliot (a writer) and Samuel Eliot (a professor), she attended the Academy of the Sacred Heart (now Doane Stuart School) in Albany, New York. She worked briefly in Boston, Massachusetts; farmed briefly in Providence, Florida; then married William Crompton and moved to the small hill town of Chesterfield, Massachusetts, where they raised five children. Anne Crompton has published twelve books, nine of them for children, including *The Snow Pony*, also from Minstrel Books. She and her husband still live in Chesterfield.

LAURIE LAWLOR

☐ THE WORM CLUB

All Arthur Cunningham wants to do is survive the last week of third grade and get picked for the fourth grade safety patrol. But when the class bully decides Arthur is his new best friend, Arthur isn't sure he'll do either!

........78900-7/$2.99

☐ ADDIE ACROSS THE PRAIRIE

"Readers will warm to Addie and her family, will find this story well-paced and exciting and will vicariously experience the trials and tribulations of the opening of the west." — *Booklist, SLJ*

...... 70147-9/$3.99

☐ ADDIE'S DAKOTA WINTER

"The 10-year-old protagonist, Addie, is greatly anticipating the beginning of the new school year, after a lonely summer with only her rough house brothers and pesky baby sister for company...."

...... 70148-7/$2.99   — *Booklist, BCCB*

☐ HOW TO SURVIVE THIRD GRADE

"Ernest Clark, a third grade outcast, thinks life is pretty miserable until a boy from Kenya enters his school... Lawlor captures the class outcast syndrome...."

...... 67713-6/$3.50   —*Booklist*

☐ ADDIE'S LONG SUMMER

Her city cousins are coming...and Addie will do anything to be friends!

...... .52607-3/$3.50

Simon & Schuster Mail Order
200 Old Tappan Rd., Old Tappan, N.J. 07675

Available from Archway Paperbacks
Published by Pocket Books

Please send me the books I have checked above. I am enclosing $_____(please add $0.75 to cover the postage and handling for each order. Please add appropriate sales tax). Send check or money order--no cash or C.O.D.'s please. Allow up to six weeks for delivery. For purchase over $10.00 you may use VISA: card number, expiration date and customer signature must be included.

Name _____

Address _____

City _____ State/Zip _____

VISA Card # _____ Exp.Date _____

Signature _____ 963A-01

WATCH OUT FOR...
BILL WALLACE

Award-winning author Bill Wallace brings you fun-filled stories of animals full of humor and exciting adventures.

- ☐ **BEAUTY** .... 74188-8/$3.50
- ☐ **RED DOG** .... 70141-X/$3.50
- ☐ **TRAPPED IN DEATH CAVE** .... 69014-0/$3.50
- ☐ **A DOG CALLED KITTY** .... 77081-0/$3.50
- ☐ **DANGER ON PANTHER PEAK** .... 70271-8/$3.50
- ☐ **SNOT STEW** .... 69335-2/$3.50
- ☐ **FERRET IN THE BEDROOM, LIZARDS IN THE FRIDGE** .... 68099-4/$3.50
- ☐ **DANGER IN QUICKSAND SWAMP** .... 70898-8/$3.50
- ☐ **CHRISTMAS SPURS** .... 74505-0/$3.50
- ☐ **TOTALLY DISGUSTING** .... 75416-5/$2.99
- ☐ **BUFFALO GAL** .... 79899-5/$3.50
- ☐ **NEVER SAY QUIT** .... 88264-3/$3.50
- ☐ **BIGGEST KLUTZ IN FIFTH GRADE** .... 86970-1/$3.50
- ☐ **BLACKWATER SWAMP** .... 51156-4/$3.50

Simon & Schuster Mail Order Dept. BWB
200 Old Tappan Rd., Old Tappan, N.J. 07675

 A MINSTREL BOOK

Please send me the books I have checked above. I am enclosing $_____ (please add $0.75 to cover the postage and handling for each order. Please add appropriate sales tax). Send check or money order--no cash or C.O.D.'s please. Allow up to six weeks for delivery. For purchase over $10.00 you may use VISA: card number, expiration date and customer signature must be included.

Name _____

Address _____

City _____ State/Zip _____

VISA Card # _____ Exp.Date _____

Signature _____

648 -13

Award-winning author
Patricia Hermes brings you:

THE COUSINS' CLUB SERIES

#1: I'LL PULVERIZE YOU, WILLIAM

Summer will never be the same for the Cousins'
Club...both creepy cousin William and an out-of-
control boa constrictor have slithered into their
vacation plans!

#2: EVERYTHING STINKS

Just one perfect day of fun—that's all that everyone
in the Cousins' Club wants. But then one incredible
event changes their very idea of perfect....

#3: THIRTEEN THINGS NOT TO
TELL A PARENT

There are all kinds of ways to have a great summer.
And most of them are going to get the Cousins'
Club in big trouble!

Available from
 A MINSTREL® BOOK

Published by Pocket Books

1097-02

MY CRAZY COUSIN COURTNEY TRILOGY
by JUDI MILLER

JOIN CATHY ON HER ADVENTURES AS SHE TRIES
TO KEEP UP WITH HER COUSIN'S CRAZY ANTICS

MY CRAZY COUSIN COURTNEY
. . . . 73821-6/$2.99US

MY CRAZY COUSIN
COURTNEY COMES BACK
. . . . 88734-3/$3.50US

MY CRAZY COUSIN
COURTNEY RETURNS AGAIN
. . . . 88733-5/$3.50US

POCKET
BOOKS

A MINSTREL® BOOK

1036-02